This   ngs to

15 MAR 2019   2 0 JUN 2019
01 APR 2019   14 SEP 2019

                                              SEP 2012

....

-7 AUG 2009   -5 JUL 2011   19 OCT 2012

                          2 2 JUL 2011
                          -6 AUG 2011   -7 DEC 2012

27 OCT   17 SEP 2011   -7 JAN 2014

2 6 MAY 2010   11 OCT 2011

        HQ   2 8 AUG 2014   -8 APR 2014   1 2 JAN 2013

Ford, Bernette   1 9 SEP 2015

Ballet class
by Bernette Ford   10 MAR 2016
and Sam Williams
            JP
                            2 8 JUN 2016
1857339   0 6 OCT 2016

For Judith K., with love and thanks,
Bernette Ford

For little dancers everywhere,
love Sam Williams

First published in hardback in Great Britain in 2008 by Boxer Books Limited.
First published in paperback in Great Britain in 2009 by Boxer Books Limited.
www.boxerbooks.com

ISBN 978-1-906250-49-2

3 5 7 9 10 8 6 4 2

Printed in Slovenia

All of our papers are sourced from managed forests and renewable resources.

Ballet Kitty
Ballet Class

Bernette Ford and Sam Williams

Boxer Books

Ballet Kitty woke up as happy as happy can be.

Her ears were pink. Her nose was pink.

And she was smiling from ear to little pink ear.

She put on her favourite pink tights and leotard,

and her new tutu and pink ballet slippers.

Today was the first day of real ballet class.

How could she wait until it was time to go?

Kitty's best friend Pussycat was

waiting outside with Ginger Tom.

Princess Pussycat had on her lilac slippers,

her lilac princess gown and cape, and of course,

her lilac jewelled crown.

Tom was wearing black shorts and a white
t-shirt, but he had trainers on his big feet.

"You can't dance in THOSE!"

said Ballet Kitty, as the three

friends arrived outside Ballet School.

"You'll trip," said Ballet Kitty.

"You'll slip," said Princess Pussycat.

"And you'll squeak," added Kitty.

"I don't care," said Ginger Tom. "I don't
want to go to ballet class, anyway!
And I WON'T wear my silly ballet shoes!"

Mademoiselle Felicity clapped her hands
and the children formed a circle.

Ballet Kitty and
Princess Pussycat
watched their teacher
and did everything
she did to warm up.

They stretched their legs.
They pointed their toes.
They raised their
arms, and shook
their hands.

But Ginger Tom was having trouble.

He couldn't stretch out his legs.

He couldn't point his toes.

When he tried to raise his arms and

stretch his hands up to the ceiling,

he fell over backward!

Princess Pussycat tried to hide a giggle.

Ballet Kitty helped him up.

Mademoiselle clapped her hands again.

Lovely piano music tinkled all around them.

Ginger Tom did much better when they all stood side by side and held the barre.

Mademoiselle showed them what to do as she called out the names of each ballet movement.

They all tried . . .

First Position

Second Position

Third Position

Fourth Position

Fifth Position

Plié

Tendu

Attitude

Curtsy

Bow

Now the ballet class moved to the

centre of the floor.

The music grew louder . . . and faster!

Ballet Kitty and Princess Pussycat held hands.

Mademoiselle Felicity took Ginger Tom's hand.

Then they followed Mademoiselle
around the room in time to the music.

They walked . . .   and skipped . . .

and ran.

Ballet Kitty had never been so happy.

Princess Pussycat had to work hard,

but she loved dancing with Ballet Kitty.

As for Ginger Tom,

he did not trip.

He did not slip.

And even though his trainers

squeaked on the shiny wood floor,

the music carried him around the room.

Ginger Tom could dance!

When the music stopped, Ballet Kitty

performed her prettiest pirouette.

Princess Pussycat curtsied.

And Ginger Tom
bent over in
a perfect bow.

There was lemonade and biscuits and cheese

at Ballet Kitty's house after ballet class.

"I can't wait till next time," said Kitty.

"Me, too," said Pussycat.

"Me, three!" said Tom, and he held up

his new ballet shoes. "And I think

next time, I'll try these out!"

Other Boxer Books paperbacks

Ballet Kitty: **Bernette Ford & Sam Williams**

A heartwarming tale of friendship and dance as Ballet Kitty and her best friend Princess Pussycat spend the day dancing and having fun. A touching and charming tale for little ballerinas everywhere.

ISBN 978-1-905417-71-1

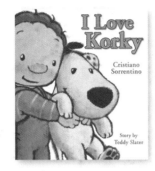

I Love Korky: **Cristiano Sorrentino**

Korky is the loveable, huggable and ever so snuggle-able puppy that all young children will adore. With appealing art and fun read-aloud text, this book is perfect for sharing with little ones.

ISBN 978-1-905417-83-4

Clip-Clop: **Nicola Smee**

When Cat, Dog, Pig and Duck climb aboard Mr Horse for a ride, they want to go faster and faster... But will "faster" lead to disaster? A delightful rhythmical text with charming illustrations which will enthral every child.

ISBN 978-1-905417-04-9

I'm Not Scared!: **Jonathan Allen**

Baby Owl is out for a moonlight stroll through the woods but each animal he bumps into tells him not to be scared! Can Baby Owl convince them that owls are supposed to be out at night and more importantly, that he is not scared?

ISBN 978-1-905417-28-5